ANIMAL
CRACKERS

PRECIOUS POTTER

ROSE IMPEY ★ SHOO RAYNER

ORCHARD BOOKS

ORCHARD BOOKS
338 Euston Road, London NW1 3BH
Orchard Books Australia
Hachette Children's Books
Level 17/207 Kent Street, Sydney NSW 2000

First published by Orchard Books in 1994
This edition published in 2009

Text © Rose Impey 1994
Illustrations © Shoo Rayner 2002

The rights of Rose Impey to be identified as the author and
Shoo Rayner to be identified as the illustrator of this Work
have been asserted by them in accordance with the
Copyright, Designs and Patents Act, 1988.

A CIP catalogue record for this book is available from the British Library.

ISBN 978 1 40830 297 2

1 3 5 7 9 10 8 6 4 2
Printed in China

Orchard Books is a division of Hachette Children's Books,
an Hachette Livre UK company.
www.hachettelivre.co.uk

Precious Potter

In Mrs Potter's litter
there were six kittens.
Well…five and a half, actually.

There was Prudence.

There was Prince

and Princess.

And there were the twins,
Pud and Pod.
That makes five.

And then there was a half.
More like a quarter, in fact.
A little scrap of fur called –
Precious.

At first Mrs Potter had to feed
Precious with an eye-dropper.

She wrapped him in a hanky.

She kept him in a box.

"That kitten will never do any good,"
said his father.
But Mrs Potter said,
"One day this cat will be famous.
You wait and see."

All her neighbours laughed –
behind their paws.

Every day Mrs Potter fed Precious
tiny little mouthfuls
with a tiny little spoon.
She called him her
tiny little sweetheart.

Soon Precious was big enough
to come out of the box
and join his brothers and sisters.
But they didn't want to play
with Precious.

Mrs Potter went on feeding Precious.
A little bit of this

and a little bit of that.

To fatten up her *little cupcake*.
Precious ate everything she gave him.
He ate and ate and ate.

In no time, Precious was as big as
his brothers and sisters.
And his appetite was growing.
When Mrs Potter put out
their bowl of food,
Precious ate as much as the rest.

But Mrs Potter went on
feeding Precious extra little titbits.
Because he had been
such a *poor little scrap*,
to begin with.

By now Precious was eating so much
the other kittens couldn't get their
share of the food.
Prudence said to her mother,
"Ma, I'm hungry.
Precious is eating everything."

But Mrs Potter ignored Prudence.
"Is my little sugar plum hungry?"
she said.

And she put out
a little plate of nibbles
for her *little treasure* to nibble.

Precious nibbled

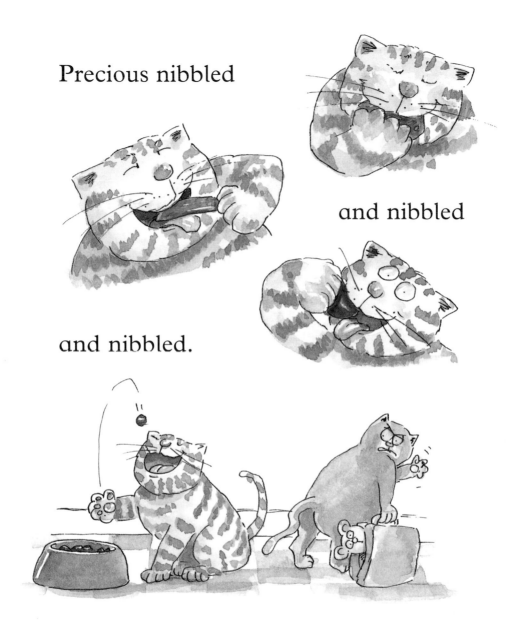

and nibbled

and nibbled.

So Prudence packed her bag and left.
But Precious was too busy eating
to notice.

Soon Precious was eating so much
Mrs Potter had to make
two bowls of food.
One for Precious
and one for the other kittens.

But the minute she turned her back
Precious ate both.

Whenever Prince and Princess
tried to get near the bowl,
Precious put out his paw
and sent them flying.
"Oh, Ma," they cried.
"Precious is such a pig!"

Mrs Potter just shook her head
and stroked Precious gently.
She said, "My little Swiss roll
has such a good appetite."

Prince and Princess packed a picnic
and left.

But Precious was too busy eating
to notice.

Precious grew bigger and bigger.
No matter how much he ate
he still felt hungry.
Even after two bowls of food,
Precious was looking round
for a little something,
to fill the corners.

Precious looked at Pud and Pod.

He licked his lips

and rolled his eyes.

Pud and Pod picked up their paws
and headed off.
"More for me," thought Precious.

At last Mr Potter noticed
how big Precious had grown.
And how much he was eating.
"Don't you think this kitten
is getting too big?" he said.

"Too big? My little marshmallow?"
said Mrs Potter. "Not at all.
In fact, I think he might need
a little more to eat."

Precious rolled
his little eyes

and licked his
little lips

and looked at Mr Potter's plate.

Mrs Potter gave Precious
his father's dinner.
Mr Potter thought
it was time to go.
Precious didn't mind.
"Just me and Ma now," he thought.

Precious had grown so big
and was so heavy
he had to have a special chair
and a special bowl

and a special bed to sleep in.

Mrs Potter could hardly afford
to feed him.

Soon there was nothing left.
Mrs Potter didn't know what to do.

"You must send Precious out
to work," said her neighbour.
"But he's such a little baby,"
said Mrs Potter.

"He's a great big lump,"
thought her neighbour.
"Anyway, if you don't,"
she said, "you'll both starve."
Mrs Potter couldn't argue with that.

So the next day
she sent Precious out to find a job.
Precious wasn't used to working.

He wasn't used to walking either.
Very slowly he walked through the
town looking for a job.

But Precious was too big
and too heavy for most jobs.
He was too heavy to be a postman.

He was too heavy to clean windows.

He was too heavy to drive a crane.

He was too heavy to fly a plane.

And he was far too heavy
to be a coal miner.

It seemed as if nobody
would give Precious a job.
Precious sat down
at the side of the road.
He was feeling very fed up.
What would he tell his ma
when he went home?

Just then someone came along
and said to Precious,
"May I introduce myself?
I am Freddy Funster.
I am the owner of
Funster's Family Circus."

Are you looking
for a job?

"It's no use," said Precious.
"I am far too big and heavy.
There is nothing I can do."
"Oh, no, you are wrong,"
said Freddy Funster.
"In my circus there is
the perfect job for you."
Precious liked the sound of that.

"What will you pay me?"
asked Precious.
"As much as you can eat,"
said the circus owner.
Precious liked the sound of that too.

So Precious joined
The Funster Family Circus as
"The Heaviest Cat in the World".

Mrs Potter was so proud of
her *little candy floss.*
"I always knew that cat
would be famous," she said.
This time none of her neighbours
laughed behind their paws.
They clapped their paws instead.

Precious Potter,
"The Heaviest Cat in the World",
ate and ate and ate
and grew bigger and bigger
and bigger...
But Mrs Potter still called him
her *little angel delight.*

Crack-A-Joke

What do you call a cat
that's just eaten a duck?
A duck-filled fatty puss!

Did you hear about the cat that
swallowed a ball of wool?
She had mittens!

What has a head like a cat, feet like a
cat, a tail like a cat, but isn't a cat?
A kitten!

The cat's whiskers!

What do you call a cat with eight legs?
An octopuss!

ANIMAL CRACKERS

COLLECT ALL THE
ANIMAL CRACKERS BOOKS!

A Birthday for Bluebell	978 1 40830 293 4	£4.99
Too Many Babies	978 1 40830 294 1	£4.99
Hot Dog Harris	978 1 40830 295 8	£4.99
Sleepy Sammy	978 1 40830 296 5	£4.99
Precious Potter	978 1 40830 297 2	£4.99
Phew Sidney	978 1 40830 298 9	£4.99
Open Wide Wilbur	978 1 40830 299 6	£4.99
We Want William	978 1 40830 300 9	£4.99

All priced at £4.99

Orchard Colour Crunchies are available from all good bookshops, or can be
ordered direct from the publisher:
Orchard Books, PO BOX 29, Douglas IM99 1BQ
Credit card orders please telephone 01624 836000
or fax 01624 837033 or visit our internet site: www.orchardbooks.co.uk
or e-mail: bookshop@enterprise.net for details.
To order please quote title, author and ISBN
and your full name and address.
Cheques and postal orders should be made payable to 'Bookpost plc.'
Postage and packing is FREE within the UK
(overseas customers should add £2.00 per book).
Prices and availability are subject to change.